THE NEW AGE

BRUTUS
THE HOUND OF
HORROR

With special thanks to Allan Frewin

www.beastquest.co.uk

ORCHARD BOOKS
338 Euston Road, London NW1 3BH
Orchard Books Australia
Level 17/207 Kent St, Sydney, NSW 2000

A Paperback Original
First published in Great Britain in 2012

Beast Quest is a registered trademark of Beast Quest Limited
Series created by Beast Quest Limited, London

Text © Beast Quest Limited 2012
Cover and inside illustrations by Steve Sims
© Beast Quest Limited 2012

A CIP catalogue record for this book is available from
the British Library.

ISBN 978 1 40831 843 0

3 5 7 9 10 8 6 4

Printed in Great Britain by CPI Group (UK) Ltd, Croydon, CR0 4YY

Orchard Books is a division of Hachette Children's Books,
an Hachette UK company

www.hachette.co.uk

BRUTUS
THE HOUND OF
HORROR

BY ADAM BLADE

ORCHARD

Henkrall

FORESTED SINKHOLE

GREAT NORTHERN MARKET

GEYSER ISLAND

I heard of Avantia in my youth, when I flew with the other children over the plains of Henkrall. They said it was a land of beauty, bravery and honour. A place of noble Beasts, too.

Even then it made me sick.

I can't fly now. My cruel mistress, Kensa, was jealous of my wings, so she took them. Don't pity me, Avantians – it's you who should be afraid. Your time is coming. Kensa has plans for your green and pleasant land. Your Good Beasts will be no defence against her servants – they'll be powerless!

You'll need more than courage to protect you from the Beasts of Henkrall!

Your sworn enemy,

Igor

PROLOGUE

"Move along there, you lazy creatures!" Old Peter's voice boomed out across the skies of Henkrall as he rode his flying donkey among the slow-moving herd of winged cattle.

He urged the donkey to fly closer to a particularly slow cow, tapping its rump with a long wooden prod. The cow mooed and its wings flapped more rapidly. The cattle around it sped up, swarming through the sky, jostling and lowing, their shadows streaking across the open countryside below.

"That's more like it!" said Old Peter. "We need to be at the Great Northern Market by midday!" He was looking forward to arriving at the gathering; there would be good trading during the day and roast meat on the spit for the evening meal. There would be dancing and laughter – even Old Peter would tumble into bed a happy man at the end of such a day!

He nudged his donkey's flanks with his heels and aimed another light tap at the nearest cow's rump. They were fine animals, bought recently from a traveller for much less than they were worth.

"I'll make a tidy profit today," he said, already imagining the weight of gold coins in his pockets.

His mood changed as he saw that

they were moving above a thick bank of fog curling across the land.

That's odd, he thought with a frown. The fog in these regions usually keeps to the mountain tops. He urged his donkey in amongst the cattle again. The sooner they were away from this fog the better.

The cattle flew on, their huge wings beating the air, their breath coming in loud snorts as they bumped together.

Old Peter's eyes narrowed in concern – tendrils of fog were reaching up towards the cattle, coiling around their necks and wings. A few of the animals began to bellow in alarm.

The herder glanced down and saw that the fog had risen to his chest. His donkey was gasping and losing height.

The fog entered his lungs, chilly

and stifling. He coughed, hearing
the frightened bellows of the cattle,
seeing their eyes roll.

What type of fog is this? He'd never come
across anything like it in all his days!

Old Peter's chest tightened, as
though steel bands were closing
around his ribs. He gulped in more of
the fog, fighting to breathe, struggling
to stay in the saddle as his donkey
bucked and tossed its head.

The fog climbed, obscuring the sky, crawling over Old Peter's skin like clammy fingers, sliding into his lungs.

He let out a gasp of fear. A shape was beginning to form at the front of the herd, where the fog was thickest.

"No!" Old Peter's voice was a weak croak, stifled by the fog. "It can't be!"

The dark shape was a pair of snapping jaws, the lips drawn back revealing deadly fangs, the gaping mouth drooling more of the fog.

As Old Peter watched, the jaws widened, letting out a monstrous, shivering howl that chilled his blood. A huge red throat was revealed as the jaws lunged forwards. Vicious fangs closed around the neck of one of the leading cattle and the animal was dragged into banks of even thicker fog, its eyes rolling back in its head.

Old Peter was too far away to help.

He heard the creature bellowing in fear as it disappeared. The noise stopped suddenly and there was the sound of slavering and chewing.

"No!" Old Peter shouted as the other cattle began to scatter in panic, crashing together as they tried desperately to escape.

Old Peter was tossed from the saddle as his donkey joined in the panic, turning in midair and beating its wings frantically. He opened his own wings, his shoulder blades stretching. He felt the breeze of his flapping wings on his face as he hung in the air, staring into the thick fog.

It began to swirl and retreat, gliding away in heavy shrouds to reveal a terrible sight. It was a gigantic winged hound, its pelt the colour of dirty gold, its teeth bloody, its lips drooling gore. The monstrous Beast's evil yellow eyes stared at Old Peter, drawing all the courage out of him.

"No! No! No!" he whimpered, his wings faltering as the Beast rose up and lunged with gaping jaws. Huge forepaws lashed out at him, and Old Peter saw that a great throbbing yellow heart beat in the Beast's chest.

Then a claw struck Old Peter and he fell, spiralling downwards.

CHAPTER ONE

NO TIME FOR REST

The town of Velora nestled in a valley high in the mountains of Henkrall. Tom and Elenna stood in the town square. All around them, townsfolk were setting up their stalls, ready to begin trading. Tom had laid his shield face-up on the ground and he was kneeling over it, gazing down at the map that had magically etched itself into the wooden surface. With one finger, he traced the glowing line of the new path that had appeared.

He knew that the winding pathway would lead them to the next stage of their Quest – to another of the deadly Beasts created by the Evil Witch Kensa.

Tom touched the two tokens they had recovered so far – Sepron's fang and Nanook's bell.

"It'll be good to have all your powers back," said Elenna. The tokens had been with them since the end of their first Quest, and each had its own magical power.

The tokens had been lost when Aduro the Good Wizard had helped Tom and Elenna travel by the Lightning Path to the world of Henkrall. It had been a dangerous journey, and one banned by the

Circle of Wizards, but Tom and Aduro had decided to take the risk for the good of Avantia.

Kensa the Witch had first appeared in Tom's kingdom while he had been at the funeral of his father. When alive, Taladon had been Avantia's Master of the Beasts. Under cover of the funeral, Kensa had stolen blood from each of the Good Beasts of Avantia, then fled back to her own realm of Henkrall.

Aduro had told Tom and Elenna that Kensa intended to create her own terrible Beasts from the earth of Henkrall and the blood of the Good Beasts. Mixing these two elements together, Kensa planned to unleash Evil Beasts on Henkrall, causing death and destruction throughout the realm. But Aduro had warned them that Kensa's ultimate goal was to bring her Beasts to Avantia.

Tom had not hesitated before deciding to enter Henkrall and defeat Kensa's Beasts. The only sadness had been that they'd had to leave Storm and Silver behind – the animals couldn't survive the lightning journey. But no sooner had they arrived in Henkrall than they had found new friends.

Tom smiled as Tempest nuzzled his shoulder. The purple horse's tawny wings were folded along his flank. Although not as noble as Storm, the valiant horse had already proved his worth many times.

Close by was his companion, the great winged wolf, Spark, grey-pelted and huge enough for Elenna to ride.

With the aid of these animals, Tom and Elenna had already defeated two of Kensa's Evil Beasts and recovered two tokens. But there were still four Beasts out there – and they had no idea what dreadful monsters they might encounter next.

"I'm not sure exactly where the path wants us to go," Tom said. The shining line had vanished under Nanook's bell. "No, wait!" he said, leaning closer. The path snaked out from under the bell and came to a halt at a small village set in the heart of the kingdom.

"There's a name!" cried Elenna, stooping forwards as bright letters appeared on the wooden surface of the shield.

Brutus.

"That must be the next Beast," said

Tom. He got to his feet, holding his shield out flat in both hands.

"I know that village," said a voice behind him.

Tom looked around. It was Harth, a stocky villager who had been suspicious of them when they'd first come here. Harth had demanded the "wingless ones" should be executed, but when Tom and Elenna had defeated the

Beast called Tarrok, the mood of the villagers had changed in their favour.

"The village hosts the Great Northern Market," Harth told them. "If you set off soon, you'll arrive in time to see one of the wondrous sights of Henkrall." He gazed up at the evening sky. "But perhaps you should take supper with us and sleep in one of our inns tonight," he offered. "You'll set off more refreshed in the morning if you do."

Tom's eyes were gritty with fatigue. A long sleep would be welcome, but then he thought back to the two Beasts he'd already encountered – Elko and Tarrok. They had been truly terrifying.

"No," he said with determination. "We need to push on while there's some light left." He glanced at Elenna who nodded her agreement.

"As you wish," said Harth.

Elenna stroked Spark. "We're leaving now," she told him. The wolf bounded about, his wings spreading and flapping. She looked at Tom, smiling. "Much as we miss Storm and Silver," she said, laughing as Spark's long tongue licked her face, "we couldn't have more faithful helpers in Henkrall!"

Tom nodded. She was right. But as he stroked Tempest's flanks, a lump filled his throat at the thought of Storm and Silver waiting patiently for them in Avantia – the kingdom he'd promised to protect.

No matter what dreadful Beasts Kensa put in his path, he wouldn't pause in his Quest. While there was

blood in his veins, he'd do everything
in his power to save both Henkrall
and Avantia!

CHAPTER TWO

WINGS OF FIRE

Evening had darkened to night and lights were shining out from the windows of Velora as Tom and Elenna prepared to depart on the next stage of their Quest. To help them in their battle with Tarrok the Blood Spike, the city elder, Pender, had given Tom and Elenna a set of wings each. They were made of leather stretched over light wooden frames, and it took a while to carefully stow them away in bags that hung from Tempest's neck.

"I'm sure they'll come in useful again," Tom said to Elenna as he mounted the small, sturdy horse. In a world where every creature could fly, the makeshift leather wings might make all the difference on their journey.

"Ready, Spark?" Elenna called, climbing onto the animal's sturdy back. The wolf barked and leapt into the air, his wings flapping.

"Come on, Tempest," said Tom, gripping his mane. The horse galloped across the courtyard, his huge tawny wings beating faster and faster. With a leap, the horse was in the air. Spark was already high in the night sky, circling the courtyard, his yellow eyes glittering and his tongue lolling as Elenna clung to the long fur around his neck.

Tom felt the horse's muscles
bunching and releasing as they flew
over the rooftops, heading into
the north. He stared ahead as they
passed between the mountain peaks,
narrowing his eyes against the chill
night wind, his hair flying.

He glanced across at Elenna and
saw anxiety in her face as Spark

flew alongside Tempest.

"It's scary, flying through the mountains in the dark," she said with an uneasy smile.

The moon was just a pale yellowy glow that came and went through the towering peaks. Tom gripped Tempest's mane more tightly, trying not to think of the jagged rocks that lurked below.

As the two animals soared on, points of white light began to sputter at the tips of their wings, spraying out in bright cascades, glowing like fireflies in the dark sky. And then the lights became silvery flames, bursting from the tips of their wings. The flames burned strong and steady, throwing out clear beams to light their way.

"Our new friends are more amazing than we thought!" laughed Tom.

"They're helping us see the way!"

Their long flight through the night seemed far less daunting now, the burning wing-tips of the two animals shining out like lanterns in the darkness.

Beneath them they could make out an occasional huddle of buildings, mountain towns and villages, shrouded in darkness.

"Most of the people are asleep down there, I expect," murmured Tom. "I wonder if any of them are having bad dreams about Kensa's Beasts?"

"I hope not," sighed Elenna. "I hate to think of this world being terrorized by that sorceress's Beasts."

Tom nodded in agreement. Two Beasts down – four to go. He had the feeling the worst of this Quest still lay ahead.

"We'll stop for a while here," said Tom, pointing to a high mountain ledge picked out by the first light of the growing dawn. They had flown through the night, and they needed to give Tempest and Spark a rest.

The ledge was narrow, only just large enough for Tempest to land on. The horse moved away from the edge, folding his wings and lowering his head to chew at some spiky blades of grass.

Spark landed and Elenna jumped off. He lay down, his head between his paws, his tongue lolling.

"I'm hungry," said Tom, wishing they had thought to bring food.

Elenna was standing on the brink of the ledge. "There's a bush growing just down there," she said, beckoning him over. "It has berries on it."

Tom stared over the ledge. The mountain fell steeply away. A spindly bush clung to the rock face, hanging with clusters of green berries. It was just within reach down the sheer side

"They're gooseberries, I think," said Tom, lying down and stretching for the fruit.

"Careful!" Elenna cried as he leant out dangerously far. "You don't have wings, remember!" She clung to his belt as he stretched down and managed to tear a cluster of the berries from the bush.

They ate hungrily despite the sour taste.

"They're not very nice," said Elenna, wiping her watering eyes. "We're going to need something a bit more filling soon."

"We'll give Tempest and Spark

a few more minutes, then we'll go," said Tom, grimacing from the berries. "Hopefully, we'll come to a village soon."

They set off into bright morning sunlight, following the path shown on Tom's shield. They had not been flying for very long when they spotted a large village ahead of them. It lay on the banks of a wide lake that sparkled in the light, but it was half-shrouded by a thin ground mist. Tom guided Tempest down in wide loops over the village.

As they drew closer, Tom saw that the village was bustling with activity. A herd of winged goats was being chased across the sky by a man riding a flying llama.

"Look at the trouble he's having with his herd," chuckled Elenna as the annoyed shouting of the goat herd wafted towards them. "I bet the farmers in Avantia don't know how easy they have it!"

They flew deeper into the mist and by the time Tempest's hooves struck firm ground on the outskirts of the town, Tom's clothes were sodden by the damp mist and his hair was hanging in his eyes.

"Oh!" gasped Elenna, climbing from Spark's back, one hand to her chest. "It's really hard...to breathe!"

"It is!" panted Tom. The mist was clammy and dank all around them. It felt as if an iron band was tightening around his chest, making every breath an effort.

They dismounted, gasping and

35

wheezing. Tempest's mouth was open
and he was snorting uncomfortably.
Spark rubbed against Elenna's legs,
looking up at her, his mouth hanging
wide as he panted.

A woman came looming out of the
mist, a tray hanging around her neck.
Her wings were spread, hung with
little vials and pouches and bottles
tied to her feathers with fine twine.
The bottles chinked and chimed
as she moved forwards. "Buy my
eucalyptus oil, friends," she cried.
"It's perfect for coughs and wheezes!"

"Thank you," said Tom, handing
over some coins and receiving a rag
soaked in eucalyptus in return.

He held the rag up so that both
he and Elenna could breathe in the
vapours. Tom's breathing became
easier, but he was worried.

"How can I fight if I can't breathe properly?" he asked Elenna. "I can't hold this rag to my face all the time. We'd better get on with this Quest while we still can!"

CHAPTER THREE

DANGER IN THE MARKETPLACE

Tom and Elenna left the two animals by the lake outside the town. In the square the market was in full swing. Taking occasional wafts of eucalyptus vapour from their rag, they made their way among the stalls.

The town was noisy and bustling as the people plied their trades. Tom could hear others coughing, and many had rags held to their faces in an attempt to keep the chilly fog out of their lungs.

"I've never seen a market quite like this," said Elenna, pointing to one of the stalls. It was loaded with hessian sacks filled with soft feathers that spilled out and fluttered lightly to the ground.

"Perfect for making wings for those special occasions!" shouted the stall-holder.

"No, thanks," said Elenna moving on with Tom to another stall where small wicker cages hung from the roof. Tiny creatures, like winged dormice, fluttered and squeaked inside.

"Let them out at night," called the woman behind the stall. "They'll circle your bed and give you the

sweetest dreams you could ever imagine!"

Tom bought them a couple of big, frothy meringues, so light that they floated in the air, and so sweet that the memory of the sour berries was banished.

"Even King Hugo's cook couldn't make these!" Elenna said, her eyes wide with pleasure.

There were sparkling, silvery drinks, too, kept in large jars that were anchored to the ground to stop them floating away. The shining liquid rose through curly glass drinking straws. Buying two of them, Tom quickly realized that you needed to keep the top of the straw between your lips to stop the delicious drink from spiraling away into the air before you could drink it.

"This world just keeps getting stranger and stranger," said Tom. "Look at that forge." He pointed to a great blacksmith's forge where the flames of a huge furnace leapt and roared beyond a wide entranceway. "It's much bigger than the forge Uncle Henry uses."

Tom bought a handful of winged yellow pears. But as the stall holder handed over the strange fruit, a frown came over his face. He was staring at something over Tom's shoulder.

Tom and Elenna turned around. The crowds had parted behind them to reveal a man Tom recognized.

"You!" the man shouted, his voice cracking. "It's all your fault!"

It was the trader who had sold Tom and Elenna Tempest and Spark.

"We've done nothing to you. What do you mean, it's my fault?" Tom called to him. He was shocked by the change in the man's appearance. His clothes were hanging from his body in tattered rags and his face was raw with claw marks. "What happened to you?"

The man brandished a cattle prod at them. "You ask me that?" he roared, turning to the crowd, his eyes wild. "You all know me – I trade in livestock! Do you wonder where my animals are now?" He pointed the stick towards Tom and Elenna. "Ask them!"

The eyes of the crowd turned towards the two friends, and now there were many hostile looks on the faces that surrounded them.

Tom heard mutterings.

"They have no wings!'

"They are strangers to this realm!"

Tom held his hands out. "We've done nothing!" he called. "Tell us what happened to your animals."

"A great Beast took them!" the man howled.

Tom felt a thrill of fear at these words. Surely he was talking about one of Kensa's Evil Beasts!

"A hound, more horrific than your worst nightmares!" the man continued, staring into Tom's face.

"It was made up of clouds of fog...
with huge yellow eyes and a great
pulsing yellow heart that could be
seen through its chest!" The man
dropped to his knees, trembling in
fear, pointing a shaking finger at Tom
and Elenna. "This all began when you
entered our kingdom! You've brought
us nothing but ill-fortune!"

"That's not true," cried Elenna.
"We're here to help you!"

"Kensa has locked herself away in
her castle," the man shouted, foam
spraying from his mouth. "There are
rumours of people going missing in
the desert!" His eyes blazed. "And
don't think I haven't seen those
two animals I sold you!"

By now, the crowd was gathered
tightly around them.

"The animals are fine," said Tom, not

understanding what the man meant.

"Exactly!" countered the trader. "They were mangy flea-bitten runts when you bought them! How did they turn into the magnificent creatures I just saw on the outskirts of the town?" His voice rose to a shriek. "You have worked sorceries on them! You are evil invaders – you steal the best of our livestock and set hideous Beasts to kill us all! You must die!"

Tom and Elenna moved closer together as the crowd closed in.

"What do we do?" Elenna whispered. Tom could feel her body trembling next to his.

He shook his head. "I have no idea," he admitted. Some of the crowd were carrying pitchforks and sticks.

It would only be a matter of moments before they attacked!

CHAPTER FOUR

THE CRUEL WHIP

"Why are you telling these lies about us?" Tom shouted.

"I'm no liar!" bellowed the man. He gestured to the crowd. "Look at them, my friends! Why is the boy armed with a sword and shield? And why does the girl have a bow and arrows?"

"We've done nothing wrong," said Tom.

"We're here to save your kingdom from Evil Beasts!" cried Elenna. "Why won't you believe us?"

"Believe wingless strangers like you?" shouted a woman in the crowd. "We'd be fools to do that."

"It's not us you should fear," Tom said. "Save your hatred for Kensa! She's the one bringing Evil Beasts to life."

Tom and Elenna backed away from the restless crowd, but still Tom didn't draw his sword. He wanted to end this confrontation with words, not sword-blows.

A commotion on the fringes of the crowd drew people's attention away. Tom heard shouts and laughter, and even the ragged trader turned to see what was going on.

A dark shape was rising and falling

in the air on the far side of the marketplace. Voices drifted on the air.

"Who's that on the flying hog?" called someone.

"One ugly hog riding another, by the look of it!" mocked another.

Tom was glad of the distraction, but he didn't like what he was hearing. *I have a bad feeling – I know who the rider is!* He saw the distant shapes swoop down towards a market stall as people ducked and dived away in alarm.

"He's stolen an apple!" cried someone. "Hey! Come back here, you dirty thief!"

Hog and rider rose back into the air – and now Tom could clearly see the deformed and hideous shape of Igor, Kensa's one-eyed hunchback minion.

Snarling and glaring with his one good eye, Igor hurled the apple

51

down at the stall holder. A moment
later, a long whip made of chain was
swinging in his hand. He sent the
hog plunging towards the crowd,
the vicious whip spinning at the
scattering people.

Igor gave a cackle. "Who will dare
taunt me now?" he croaked. "Who is
brave enough to do battle with Igor?"
The whip snaked and cracked as the

hog soared over the fleeing crowds.

"The boy stranger will fight you!" shouted the trader, pointing towards Tom. "He has a sword! Clear a space for him, my friends. Let him do battle."

Before he knew what was happening, Tom found the crowd dividing and backing away, leaving a clear space between him and the hunchback. Igor was now hovering above the marketplace, the whip whirling above his head.

"Take him on, boy!" shouted a voice. "Cut him and his hog into bacon slices!"

Tom glanced around to see Elenna struggling in the crowd. They were doing her no harm, but they held her back, as though they wanted to see Tom fight the hunchback alone.

Igor's eye glittered with delight. "Let the duel commence!" he shouted, urging his hog forwards, the long whip scything the air.

Tom only just had time to draw his sword and lift his shield before the hunchback was on him. The chain whip clanked loudly as it struck his shield, but before Tom could fight back, the hog had veered off and risen into the air again, snorting loudly and kicking its trotters.

From the corner of his eye, Tom saw that Elenna had broken away from the mass of spectators and had taken a position behind some barrels. She had an arrow on the bowstring, ready to shoot at Igor if the battle went badly.

Igor came plunging down again, snarling and swinging his whip.

Tom lunged at him, but the hog flew
quickly upwards as the cruel whip
raked across Tom's back, almost
knocking him over.

"Fight harder!" shouted someone.
"The ugly little toad is making a fool
of you!'

Tom gritted his teeth. He had to

end this quickly!

Once more the hog hurtled downwards, but this time Tom was ready. He lifted his sword, holding it firmly in two hands as the whip snaked forwards, catching on the blade and winding around it.

Setting his feet firmly apart, Tom dragged at the tangled whip. With a squeal of horror, Igor was wrenched from the hog. He came thumping down on his bent back as his animal shot up into the sky.

"Get him!" called a voice in the crowd. "Get him before he can get up."

Igor grovelled on the ground, his hand over his face, whimpering in fear.

"Don't hurt me!" he cried, his stunted legs kicking feebly. "I was only fooling around." His tear-stained face stared pitifully up at Tom. "You must believe me, I would never have hurt you."

Tom pulled his sword loose from the whip and turned away.

"Watch out!" he heard Elenna cry.

But it was too late. Igor sent his whip slashing through the air, catching Tom hard across his thighs. The force took his feet out from under him.

Tom crashed to the ground, his legs burning with pain.

"To me!" Igor cackled to his hog, which plunged down so that in an instant Igor was back in the saddle, the whip swinging around his head.

Tom staggered to his feet, but his legs were unsteady and he had to lean on his sword to stop himself from falling. The hog was flying upwards again – in a moment, Igor would be out of reach. Tom's fighting instincts took over. He leapt up, stretching out his sword so that the tip of the blade cut the strap around the hog's belly, slicing it cleanly in two.

For a moment, Igor hung in the slipping saddle, his arms flailing. Then he fell, crashing to the ground, his legs kicking.

Tom was on him in a moment, twirling his sword so that the whip was tangled in its blade once more. But this time he jerked back, wrenching the whip out of Igor's hand and sending it flying.

With a squeal of anger, Igor struggled to his feet. Snatching up his whip, he darted away into the crowd.

An arrow from Elenna sped after him, scratching his arm and making him yell with fright and anger.

"You coward!" called Tom, as Igor forced his way through the startled crowd. "You won't get away that easily." He chased after the fleeing hunchback, hearing Elenna's rapid footsteps close behind him.

"Stop them!" howled the ragged trader. "The hunchback is in league with the two wingless strangers. This was all a ploy to help them escape!"

The crowd surged forwards, blocking Tom and Elenna's way. Between the people, Tom caught a glimpse of the lumbering shape of the hunchback darting away. Igor was escaping!

CHAPTER FIVE

THE FOUL MARSH

"Get back!" Tom shouted, swinging his sword in a wide arc as the crowd moved towards him and Elenna. "I don't want to hurt anyone, but I need to catch that man."

Elenna had run to his side, an arrow ready in her bow.

Muttering darkly, the people drew back, leaving a clear path out of the marketplace.

The two friends raced off in pursuit of Igor.

The hunched shape darted away between buildings, moving quickly on his stumpy legs. Every now and then he would glance back, a sneer on his ugly face.

Almost as if he's luring us out of the town on purpose, Tom thought. His fist tightened around his sword hilt. "We must be ready for anything," he told Elenna.

She nodded, eyes gleaming.

Beyond the edge of the town, the fog swirled more thickly, almost as dense as water, clogging their lungs. Tom offered the eucalyptus-soaked rag to Elenna, then breathed in its fumes himself.

They had entered a dank stretch of flat marshland. A dull, leaden twilight

was falling, making it even harder
to see what lay ahead.

There was no sign of Igor. Had he
led them to this desolate place for
some dreadful purpose of his own?
Was it a trap?

Flickering spurts of marsh-gas licked
upwards on the edge of Tom's sight,
ghostly through the coils of fog.

He looked up at the sound of wings
beating above their heads. The fog
swept away to reveal Tempest and
Spark hovering in the air. Bright
flames burned again at their wingtips,
shedding light onto the gloomy
marsh.

"They followed us!" cried Elenna.
"They must have sensed we'd need
them."

"Thank you!" Tom called up. He
pointed into the marsh. "We need

63

to go deeper in – will you light our way?"

Although they could not understand human speech, they seemed to instinctively know what Tom and Elenna needed. Flapping slowly through the darkening sky, they moved on into the marsh, lighting up the land below.

Tom stepped forwards, his feet

sinking into wet slime. All around him, marsh-lights danced like twisting ghouls over pools of oily scum.

A howling moan rang through the fog, sending cold shivers down Tom's spine. He glanced at Elenna. "That was Brutus, for sure!" he muttered, remembering the Beast's name that had appeared on his shield.

"Igor lured us here to be killed," said Elenna.

Tom nodded. "Then more fool him," he said grimly. "The sooner we meet the Beast, the better."

Guided by the wing-tip lights of Tempest and Spark, Tom and Elenna made their way deeper and deeper into the oozy marsh. Igor had disappeared, but surely the Beast had to be out here somewhere? All the while, the fog grew thicker, until it felt to Tom as though they were pushing against a wall of choking water.

They shared the rag, hardly able to suck the dense air into their lungs, choking on the growing stench.

"What is that stink?" gasped Elenna, her eyes screwed up, the rag to her nose.

"It smells like the wet pelt of some filthy dog," coughed Tom. "A wet dog that's been rolling in rotting cabbage!"

At that moment, the fog that draped over them like a blanket began to move. Tom let out a gasp as a shape took form in the murk. Spark let out an anxious whine above Tom's head.

Suddenly, the dark shape lunged forwards, sending Tom spinning sideways. He fell into one of the oily marsh pools, making the ghoulish lights leap and flicker.

There was a hiss of flying arrows as Elenna shot shaft after shaft at the huge dark shape.

Tom leapt to his feet, staring up as the dreadful form took to the air. Tempest and Spark fled in fear as the hideous form of a gigantic hound hovered over the marsh, his huge wings beating slowly, sending a suffocating stink. The Beast stared down, his yellow eyes filled with hatred and wickedness. Spittle drooled from slathering jaws. His pelt was a dirty gold colour and his long claws curled into vicious points.

Just like the claws of Epos! Tom realized.

This was Brutus, a Beast made from the blood of Avantia's Flame Bird. Tom stared up at the hovering

monster. In the Beast's chest, a
glowing yellow heart throbbed
through the tangled hair. To defeat

Brutus he would have to steal that pulsing heart.

But how was he going to get close enough?

CHAPTER SIX

MAD DOGS

With a terrible howl, Brutus plunged
towards Tom, jaws gaping as he
belched out more of the stinking fog.

At the last moment, Tom leapt
aside, the fangs grazing his shoulder
as the Beast swept past him. He
turned, aiming a blow at the Beast's
flank. But the moment before
the blade struck flesh, the hound
dissolved into fog again.

Tom stumbled forwards, falling to his knees in the soft mire. Brutus was already climbing into the air again, wings flapping powerfully.

Grimacing, Tom got to his feet as the Beast turned and dived down again, yellow eyes gleaming, curved claws reaching.

Tom struck out with his shield, but he was beaten back by the impact of the claws. It was almost impossible to get a firm footing in the marsh and the moment he swung his sword at the Beast's outstretched leg, fur and flesh evaporated into fog. He tumbled forwards, the oily water splashing up around him, the ghost-lights flaring, the air wheezing in his chest.

He heard the swish of arrows as Elenna joined battle with the Beast, but although her aim was true, the shafts found only swathes of fog where the body of Brutus had been a moment before.

Now the Beast came gliding towards Tom, close to the ground, wreathed in mist so that only his claws and eyes and the beating heart could be clearly seen.

How can I fight a Beast that fades into fog the moment I try to hit it? Then, Tom had a desperate idea.

He stood firm this time, allowing the howling Beast to bear down on him. *Come and get me!* he thought. He flung his shield-arm up towards the fangs. The teeth closed on the shield's wooden rim. The Beast shook his head, like a giant dog playing with a bone. Tom was thrown dizzyingly from side to side, his arms feeling as though they could be torn from their sockets, but he reached out and – yes!

– managed to thrust his sword into
the Beast's mouth.

He struck flesh this time! Howling in
pain, Brutus dissolved into fog before
the blade could sink deeper. The fight
was turning in Tom's favour – just.

But then Brutus hurtled up into the

air, giving out blood-curdling howls.

"Well done, Tom!" cried Elenna, staring upwards. "Is the Beast giving up?"

"I don't think so," said Tom. The hairs on his arms stood up straight as Brutus let out another howl. Something wasn't right here. "Listen!"

From the direction of the town, they could hear howling and barking, the noise getting rapidly louder.

Tom finally understood. "He's calling all the town's dogs to him!"

Moments later, they saw the dark shapes of the onrushing dogs looming out of the fog.

"Keep them off, but try not to hurt them," cried Tom. "The Beast is making them behave like this."

The dogs hurtled forwards, drooling and snapping their jaws, their eyes filled with an evil light – just like the Beast whose will had possessed them. As the dogs surrounded him and Elenna, Tom did his best to use the flat of his blade to beat them off, and Elenna's arrows were aimed to frighten rather than injure.

They could hear Brutus letting out triumphant howls as they battled against the raging dogs. Sharp teeth snapped and claws raked at them as Tom and Elenna struggled to fight off the pack of maddened animals. Hard as they fought, they couldn't prevent teeth and claws from tearing their clothes.

How could they defeat so many enemies? And how soon before Brutus attacked again? Tom looked up. Tempest and Spark were diving and soaring through the air, drawing the Beast's attention away. But Brutus was growing angrier and more dangerous by the second. Tom had to do something quickly to get rid of the wild dogs. He glanced at the marsh-flames, an idea forming in his mind.

"Tear strips from your sleeves," he called to Elenna. "Then tie the cloth around your arrows and set them alight! Fire will scare the dogs away!"

Elenna nodded. While Tom continued fighting, she ripped some cloth from her tunic and bound it tightly around an arrow. She dipped it into a flame. It caught fire, and she shot it towards the dogs. They cowered away from the flames, yelping and yapping.

"It's working!" Elenna shouted, wrapping another arrow and holding it in the flame. She shot it towards the pack and they leapt this way and that, howling in fear as they tumbled over one another to avoid the flames.

A great roar of anger sounded from above them. Brutus was plunging towards them, his eyes blazing.

"Aim at the heart!" Tom shouted.

An arrow sped upwards, but the Beast turned aside at the last moment and the flaming arrow caught his thick pelt instead. The long tangled fur shriveled away from the burning point of the arrow. But then, Brutus turned into fog again and the fire died as the arrow fell away.

Tom caught hold of Elenna's arm and pulled her behind a long mound of moss. "Fire is the way to defeat it!" he gasped. "But your arrows aren't going to be enough."

"Then what shall we do?" asked Elenna.

Tom's eyes narrowed as he remembered something. "The forge in the town has a huge furnace," he said. "We have to lure the Beast to it!"

"What about the people there?" gasped Elenna.

Tom gave her a steely look. "We'll do everything we can to stop the Beast from harming them," he said. "But the only way to defeat this creature is with a massive fire."

They looked into each other's eyes. This was the only choice they had.

CHAPTER SEVEN

FOG AND FLAME

Tom sprang to his feet, calling and waving his sword into the night sky.

"Tempest! Spark! To us!" he shouted.

The two animals were high in the sky, their wing-tip flames shining through the fog like burning comets.

All around Tom and Elenna, the hounds were circling and howling, their fearful eyes on the burning arrow that Elenna had trained on them.

Tempest swooped down, neighing fiercely, legs stretched out ready to land. But the dogs twisted around as they heard him, their eyes shining at the sight of new prey. The pack surged towards Tempest, barking and slavering. The horse flapped his wings and took to the air again, as the dogs leapt and snapped at his hooves.

Spark hovered above the dogs, growling. There were too many dogs for even a wolf as big and brave as him to fight.

"We have to get to higher ground!" gasped Tom, already running towards a slime-covered green rock that jutted up from the swirling fog.

They ran, Elenna's arrow still aimed

towards the pack of dogs.

A little way off, a huge dark shape swept through the fog on wide wings. Yellow eyes flared with malice. Terrible growls made the ground beneath their feet tremble.

Brutus was coming for them again.

Slithering and slipping, the two friends clambered up onto the wet rock. From here, they might be able to get to their animal companions. There was only just room for both of them to stand on its high ridge. Tempest and Spark flew down towards them.

"You go first!" shouted Tom.

Elenna loosed the last of her burning arrows at Brutus, then scrambled up onto her flying wolf's back.

The dogs were hurling themselves

at the rock, their fangs grazing Tom's legs as he flung himself up, snatching at Tempest's mane and heaving himself onto his back.

"To the town!" Tom shouted to Tempest, whistling between his teeth. Tempest soared upwards, Spark at his side. The furious howling of the mad dogs fell away beneath them.

Spark and Tempest flew in a wide arc, turning towards the faint lights of the town.

The ghastly fog thinned as they flew away. Tom looked back, his eyes stinging in the rushing air. A fearsome shape rose from the marsh. Tom smiled grimly – his plan was working, Brutus was following them.

Clinging on, Tom guided Tempest down between the buildings of the town, making for the marketplace.

Spark and Elenna were close behind.
It was dark now, and the town was
alight with torches and fires as the
people continued their business into
the night.

Tom heard howls behind him,
followed by crashing sounds. He
glanced back and saw Brutus hurtling
after them at rooftop height, the
Beast's huge wings smashing into
houses, sending roof tiles and
stonework spinning through the air,

leaving a path of destruction in its wake.

As Tempest and Spark swept over the marketplace, the people stared up, shouting and pointing and shaking their fists at Tom and Elenna. But their shouts turned to screams of terror as Brutus came bursting into the marketplace, drooling thick, stinking fog from between his gaping jaws.

The people turned stalls over in their rush to escape the Beast. Tom leant forwards, guiding Tempest down towards the forge. The horse came to a cantering halt at the entrance. Tom and Elenna leapt off their animals, coming down into waist-deep fog that rolled like slime across the ground as Brutus swooped low.

"Get away from here!" Tom shouted

to Tempest and Spark. The two animals took to the air, flying away from Brutus.

Tom stood at the wide entrance of the forge, brandishing his sword. "Do your worst!" he shouted at the onrushing Beast.

With an ear-splitting roar, Brutus thrust his great head in through the entrance, his jaws closing, fangs clashing. But Tom jumped back, making his stand between the hideous hound and the leaping flames of the furnace.

"Come on!" Tom taunted the Beast, waving his sword. "What are you waiting for?"

Brutus surged forwards, his wings smashing into the walls on either side of the entrance. Wood and stone flew through the air. Tom saw Elenna

circling around the Beast's head, a
flaming arrow on her bow, lit from
the furnace fires.

Brutus furled his wings and pushed
deeper into the forge, eyes burning
as brightly as the furnace fires, his
nostrils spurting wet, stinking steam.

Tom sprang back again, taunting
the Beast, forcing him to push deeper
into the forge, closer to the furnace.

There was doubt in the yellow eyes now, and an uneasy tremor in the Beast's growling. He knew the fire was dangerous. Brutus paused, glaring at Tom. He came no closer to the furnace.

My plan's not working! Tom thought desperately. "Whilst there's blood in my veins," he muttered, "I'll get this Beast into the fire."

He saw Elenna slide along the wall, flanking the Beast, a burning arrow at the ready. She shot the arrow at Brutus's neck, then leapt forwards, clutching at the golden fur, climbing high onto the Beast's back.

Roaring, Brutus twisted and turned, his claws scrabbling and fangs snapping as he tried to bite at the burning arrow and shake Elenna off.

The wings spread again, smashing

into the walls of the forge. As the Beast writhed, he crashed into the wooden posts that held the roof up. Tom dived aside as great chunks of roofing began to tumble down. The forge was being broken to pieces.

"No!" shouted Tom as Elenna lost her grip on the Beast's back and went crashing to the ground.

If the forge was wrecked, the Beast would escape again and Tom's plan would be ruined.

Brutus rose up, smashing through the roof, howling in triumph as the forge fell to pieces. Tom leapt back from the falling debris, but a roof beam struck him and sent him crashing to the ground dangerously close to the furnace flames.

Agony seared through his shoulder and back as he struggled to lift the

beam. But it was too heavy for him.
He lay gasping for breath as the
blazing heat of the furnace began
to singe his hair and clothes.

*This is the end! I'll die here and Brutus
will triumph!*

CHAPTER EIGHT

SHADOWS AND SWORDS

Tom could smell his clothes smouldering as he lay trapped under the fallen roof-beam. His heart was pounding and he could hardly draw breath in the stinking fog. He lifted a hand to wipe the sweat out of his eyes.

While I'm lying here helpless, what mayhem is Brutus causing? Tom thought.

He saw Elenna running to and fro,

jumping lumps of cracked masonry and hurdling pieces of the ruined roof as Brutus's fangs snapped at her heels. But the wreckage was working in Elenna's favour. Brutus was too big and too slow to catch her easily.

Tom watched Brutus in frustration, feeling sure that the Beast was smaller than before – the furnace heat was having an effect on Kensa's monster. If only Tom could get free, he might have a chance!

Elenna snatched up a sword. "If you've hurt Tom, I'll make you pay!" she shouted, thrusting and lunging with the sword, fending off the scything claws as she danced in and around the wreckage.

Tom saw her shadow leaping on the broken walls. If only he could help her!

The shadow!

That was the answer.

Tom managed to work his hand beneath his body, his muscles screaming with pain. He touched Kaymon's white diamond, attached to his belt. As his fingers closed around the diamond, he felt his own shadow slip out from under him. It leapt up, prancing back and forth in front of him.

Tom was frozen now that he was separated from his shadow, but he shifted his glance to where a new-forged sword stood against the wall, its shadow dark behind it.

"Take the shadow sword!" he commanded his shadow. "Fight the Beast for me!"

The Tom-outline sprang to the sword and swept up its shadow, brandishing it wildly as it ran through the ruins towards Brutus.

The Beast had Elenna cornered at last, his foul breath wreathing in thick tendrils around her as she bravely swung the sword she had picked up.

Tom could hardly bear to look as the Beast's jaws widened and

a victorious howl rang across the marketplace.

Go, shadow, go... Tom silently willed, his teeth gritted.

The shadow-Tom jumped up behind the Beast and struck it hard on the flank with his sword. Howling in rage, Brutus spun around, his yellow eyes glaring.

The shadow-Tom thumbed its nose as it pranced away, leaping lightly over the fallen timbers, the sword whirling in its hand.

Brutus hurtled forwards, but his vicious claws struck against the wall as the nimble shadow bounded away again, its mouth wide open in silent laughter.

Again and again, Brutus flung himself at the taunting shadow, but each time, the dark shape would

bounce out of reach, often with a
painful thrust or swipe of the shadow
sword as it went, making the Beast
roar with anger and frustration.

Elenna joined in the battle again,
stabbing at the Beast then racing away.

"Catch me if you can!" she jeered, ducking behind a broken chunk of wall as Brutus veered from side to side, letting out howls of rage as he tried to trap one of his swift-footed attackers.

Tom groaned as he watched Elenna and his shadow battling the Beast. Although they were fighting well, neither of them seemed able to defeat Brutus. Only with Tom's help would Kensa's Beast be vanquished. But Tom lay trapped, pinned down by the agonizing pressure of the fallen timbers across his legs. Not that he would have been able to go to Elenna's aid while his shadow was active.

He had to take a risk before the heat of the leaping furnace grew so fierce that he passed out!

"Shadow, to me!" he called.

The shadow came forwards, sliding quickly under Tom. Able to move freely again, Tom strained his painful muscles as he pushed up against the fallen beam of wood that was holding him down.

He could hear Brutus snarling as the Beast hunted for Elenna among the ruins.

Sweat poured from Tom's face as he heaved upwards, but the enforced break from battle had refreshed him a little, and he felt the beam shifting above him. Straining with every sinew in his body, Tom managed to slip from under the beam and stagger to his feet. His clothes were smoking and he was so hot from the furnace fire that he was becoming dizzy.

He stumbled forwards, his head

spinning, his sight blurring as the world span around him. He couldn't pass out – not now!

CHAPTER NINE

THE FIRES OF DEATH

Tom was about to lose consciousness, when he spotted a wooden bucket brimming with water standing alongside the furnace wall. He staggered towards it and stooped, using the last of his strength to lift it from the ground and heave it up above his head.

He upended the bucket and felt the

cooling water flood down over his head and body. Gasping and spitting water, Tom threw the bucket aside. His head was clear now. It was time for the final fight!

He could see the great winged shape of the Beast towering over Elenna as she held her sword up bravely, her back to a broken section of the forge's outer wall. A huge paw rose, the claws spreading, ready to tear at her, to crush her to the ground and kill her.

"Brutus!" Tom shouted, leaping up onto the wall of the furnace and brandishing his sword. He could feel the fires raging at his back. He could feel his clothes smouldering again, the water he had thrown over himself turning into steam in the intense heat.

"I'm your real enemy!" Tom shouted so loudly that he felt as if he was shredding his throat. "Come and get me! Or are you just a big wet dog after all?"

The Beast's head turned, the lips curling back from the drooling fangs, his eyes ferocious with anger.

"Bad doggie!" Tom taunted.

Brutus let out a howl of fury, spinning around in the debris of the forge. With another roar, he leapt at Tom, claws glinting like razors in the red furnace light, jaws gaping as though he meant to swallow Tom in one great gulp.

At the very last moment, Tom flung himself aside, springing down to the ground and rolling away from the furnace.

But the Beast was moving too fast to stop itself! With a terrible, shivering howl, Brutus crashed head-first into the furnace. A great fountain of steam exploded into the

air as the Beast was swallowed by
the flames. For a moment, Tom saw
the misty shape of the Beast writhing
in the fire, shrinking away, giving
out chilling howls that dwindled to a
hissing crackle. And then it was gone.

Another noise broke out even as Brutus was consumed by the flames. It was the maddened barking and howling of a pack of dogs. Tom spun around. The town dogs were still under the Beast's evil spell! Now they were attacking the forge, leaping in over the broken walls, hunting for their prey.

Elenna came racing over to Tom and the two friends stood side by side in the forge, their swords ready. The defeat of Brutus was not the end of the battle.

As the slavering and howling dogs advanced, Tom saw Tempest and Spark fly towards them. The brave wolf snapped at the dogs, and Tempest's hooves kicked at them.

"Drive them off!" shouted Tom, leaping forwards with Elenna at his side. They lunged at the dogs, still trying to avoid hurting them as they pushed forwards, swinging their swords and shouting.

The fight did not last long. Attacked by cold steel and hard hooves, the pack split up and fled, howling and whining into the night.

Tempest and Spark landed, folding their wings and moving close to Tom and Elenna under the jutting remains of the forge's high roof.

"Thank you," Elenna gasped, stroking Spark's fur. "We might not have been able to fend them off without your help."

Tom leant on his sword, catching his breath as he watched the dogs streaming away across the marketplace.

"Poor things," said Elenna. "It's not their fault."

"The spell that's making them wild should wear off quickly now," Tom said. He turned and stared back at the furnace. The flames were lower, flickering among the coals as though the effort of dissolving Brutus had taken most of the life out of the fire.

But Brutus was gone – gone for good. In the heart of the fire, Tom saw the yellow jewel that had been the Evil Beast's heart. And lying in the embers close to it was Epos's talon.

Tom stepped towards the fire, his trusty sword in his hand. The heat was still fierce, and he held his shield up to protect himself as he reached with his sword deep into the furnace. He used the tip of the blade to rake the jewel and the talon to the edge of the fire.

They fell to the ground, tendrils of smoke rising from them.

Elenna came up behind him. She had found another bucket of water. She handed it to Tom and he dashed the water over the jewels and the talon.

There was a hiss and a rush of steam as the cold water hit the two strange, magical items.

Tom crouched and tentatively touched the talon. It was cool. Smiling, he turned his shield face up and put Epos's talon back in its place. He would be able to use its healing powers now to close wounds.

He picked up the yellow jewel that had been Brutus's beating heart and pushed it into his tunic, meaning to keep it safe.

As he turned, he heard an ominous creaking from above. He stared upwards. The shattered remains of the roof were poised above them, the heavy beams unsupported now, bending under the weight of the slates.

With a sudden rush and rumble, the beams gave way and the roof came crashing down towards them.

CHAPTER TEN

THE DANGER NEVER ENDS

Whinnying in fright, Tempest spread his wings and took to the air as the roof caved in on them. Tom caught hold of Elenna's hand, snatching at Tempest's mane as the horse soared into the air. His feet were torn from the ground as Tempest flew upwards. He kept a tight grip on Elenna's hand, the sinews and muscles of his arms

and shoulders straining with the
effort.

As they rose, Tom heard the crunch
and boom of the falling roof. He
glanced back and saw Spark flying
close behind through the billowing
smoke.

Tempest swooped lower as he flew across the marketplace. Tom saw that Elenna's dangling feet were close to the ground. He released her and she landed neatly, Spark at her side.

Tom heaved himself up on Tempest's back as the horse came to land. The forge was a complete ruin now, a few flames flickering in the wreckage as plumes of dark smoke rose into the night sky.

People began to emerge from among the buildings that ringed the marketplace. The faces of the townsfolk were shocked and bewildered, but it was clear from their behaviour that they no longer suspected Tom and Elenna of being their enemies.

"Do you trust us now?" Tom called. "I'm on your side. The only reason

we came to your kingdom was
to defeat Kensa's Beasts!"

The ragged trader stepped out of
the crowd that now surrounded the
four companions. "I am sorry I spoke
against you," he said. "You have
saved us from certain death."

There were murmurs of agreement
from the other townsfolk.

"The danger is not over," Tom
warned them. "There will be more
Beasts." He raised his voice so they
could all hear him. "If you want to
know the truth of what's happening,
you should send some people to
Kensa's castle."

"We will do that," said a tall, dark-
eyed man, stepping forwards. "I will
go, and I'll take a few stout-hearted
fellows with me. If Kensa has turned
on her own people, we will find out

why!" His eyes flashed. "Will you and your companions go with us?"

Tom looked gravely at the man. "It's good to have made new friends here," he said. "But I have to continue on my Quest – there are three more Beasts to defeat before the danger to your realm is averted." *And the threat to my kingdom is conquered,* he thought.

The trader stepped closer, looking up into Tom's face. "I am ashamed to have doubted you," he said. "Is there anything we can do to help you on your way?"

"You could supply us with food and water for our travels," said Elenna.

"That will be done!" said another of the townsfolk. "It's the least we can offer."

Tom patted Tempest's neck. The sturdy little horse had saved their lives when the forge's roof had collapsed. But did he really want to lead the brave animal into yet more danger?

He looked down, seeing how Spark rubbed up against Elenna, his eyes glowing with friendship as she threw her arms around his neck.

Tom had the feeling that even if they tried to leave their two animals friends behind, Tempest and Spark would follow them, no matter how dangerous the Quest became.

Townsfolk offered bags of food and drink that Tom stuffed in his pockets. Elenna climbed onto Spark's back.

"Good speed," called many of the people. "Fare you well!"

"And you!" said Tom, gripping his horse's mane and giving a low whistle. Tempest's ears twitched.

The animal rose on its hind legs, whinnying loudly. People moved away as Tempest cantered across the marketplace, his wings spreading.

A moment later, he was flying over the town, Spark soaring along at his side.

Tom and Elenna waved down one final time at the cheering people as the town fell away behind them.

As they flew over the marshes, Tom's mind began to fill with thoughts of what was to come. What kind of terrible Beast would Kensa's evil sorceries conjure up next?

He gritted his teeth, his fingers tightening around Tempest's purple mane. Whatever appalling monsters lurked in their path, he would do everything in his power to defeat them and bring peace to the land of Henkrall.

That was his promise!

Join Tom on the next stage
of the Beast Quest when he meets

FLAYMAR
THE SCORCHED
BLAZE

Win an exclusive
Beast Quest T-shirt and goody bag!

Tom has battled many fearsome Beasts and we want to know which one is your favourite! Send us a drawing or painting of your favourite Beast and tell us in 30 words why you think it's the best.

Each month we will select **three** winners to receive a Beast Quest T-shirt and goody bag!

Send your entry on a postcard to
BEAST QUEST COMPETITION
Orchard Books, 338 Euston Road, London NW1 3BH.

Australian readers should email:
childrens.books@hachette.com.au

New Zealand readers should write to:
Beast Quest Competition, PO Box 3255, Shortland St,
Auckland 1140, NZ or email: childrensbooks@hachette.co.nz

**Don't forget to include your name and address.
Only one entry per child.**

Good luck!

1. Ferno the Fire Dragon
2. Sepron the Sea Serpent
3. Arcta the Mountain Giant
4. Tagus the Horse-Man
5. Nanook the Snow Monster
6. Epos the Flame Bird

Beast Quest:
The Golden Armour
7. Zepha the Monster Squid
8. Claw the Giant Monkey
9. Soltra the Stone Charmer
10. Vipero the Snake Man
11. Arachnid the King of Spiders
12. Trillion the Three-Headed Lion

Beast Quest:
The Dark Realm
13. Torgor the Minotaur
14. Skor the Winged Stallion
15. Narga the Sea Monster
16. Kaymon the Gorgon Hound
17. Tusk the Mighty Mammoth
18. Sting the Scorpion Man

Beast Quest:
The Amulet of Avantia
19. Nixa the Death Bringer
20. Equinus the Spirit Horse
21. Rashouk the Cave Troll
22. Luna the Moon Wolf
23. Blaze the Ice Dragon
24. Stealth the Ghost Panther

Beast Quest:
The Shade of Death
25. Krabb Master of the Sea
26. Hawkite Arrow of the Air
27. Rokk the Walking Mountain
28. Koldo the Arctic Warrior
29. Trema the Earth Lord
30. Amictus the Bug Queen

Beast Quest:
The World of Chaos
31. Komodo the Lizard King
32. Muro the Rat Monster
33. Fang the Bat Fiend
34. Murk the Swamp Man
35. Terra Curse of the Forest
36. Vespick the Wasp Queen

Beast Quest:
The Lost World
☐ 37. Convol the Cold-Blooded Brute
☐ 38. Hellion the Fiery Foe
☐ 39. Krestor the Crushing Terror
☐ 40. Madara the Midnight Warrior
☐ 41. Ellik the Lightning Horror
☐ 42. Carnivora the Winged Scavenger

Beast Quest:
The Pirate King
☐ 43. Balisk the Water Snake
☐ 44. Koron Jaws of Death
☐ 45. Hecton the Body Snatcher
☐ 46. Torno the Hurricane Dragon
☐ 47. Kronus the Clawed Menace
☐ 48. Bloodboar the Buried Doom

Beast Quest:
The Warlock's Staff
☐ 49. Ursus the Clawed Roar
☐ 50. Minos the Demon Bull
☐ 51. Koraka the Winged Assassin
☐ 52. Silver the Wild Terror
☐ 53. Spikefin the Water King
☐ 54. Torpix the Twisting Serpent

Beast Quest:
Master of the Beasts
☐ 55. Noctila the Death Owl
☐ 56. Shamani the Raging Flame
☐ 57. Lustor the Acid Dart
☐ 58. Voltrex the Two-Headed Octopus
☐ 59. Tecton the Armoured Giant
☐ 60. Doomskull the King of Fear

Special Bumper Editions
☐ Vedra & Krimon: Twin Beasts of Avantia
☐ Spiros the Ghost Phoenix
☐ Arax the Soul Stealer
☐ Kragos & Kildor: The Two-Headed Demon
☐ Creta the Winged Terror
☐ Mortaxe the Skeleton Warrior
☐ Ravira, Ruler of the Underworld
☐ Raksha the Mirror Demon
☐ Grashkor the Beast Guard

All books priced at £4.99.
Special bumper editions priced at £5.99.

Orchard Books are available from all good bookshops, or can be ordered from our website: www.orchardbooks.co.uk, or telephone 01235 827702, or fax 01235 8227703.

Series 11: THE NEW AGE
COLLECT THEM ALL!

A new land, a deadly enemy and six new Beasts await Tom on his next adventure!

978 1 40831 841 6

978 1 40831 842 3

978 1 40831 843 0

978 1 40831 844 7

978 1 40831 845 4

978 1 40831 846 1

Meet six terrifying new Beasts!

Solak, Scourge of the Sea
Kajin the Beast Catcher
Issrilla the Creeping Menace
Vigrash the Clawed Eagle
Mirka the Ice Horse
Kama the Faceless Beast

**Watch out for the next
Special Bumper
Edition**

SPECIAL
BUMPER
EDITION!

THE CHRONICLES OF AVANTIA

FROM THE DARK, A HERO ARISES...

Dare to enter the kingdom of Avantia.

A new evil arises in Avantia. Lord Derthsin has
ordered his armies into the four corners of
Avantia. If the four Beasts of Avantia can
find their Chosen Riders they might have the
strength to challenge Derthsin. But if they fail,
the land of Avantia will be lost forever...

FIRST HERO, CHASING EVIL, CALL TO WAR, FIRE AND FURY—OUT NOW!

Read on for an exclusive extract of
CEPHALOX THE CYBER SQUID!

The Merryn's Touch

The water was up to Max's knees and still rising. Soon it would reach his waist. Then his chest. Then his face.

I'm going to die down here, he thought.

He hammered on the dome with all his strength, but the plexiglass held firm.

Then he saw something pale looming through the dark water outside the submersible. A long, silvery spike. It must be the squid-creature, with one of its weird robotic attachments. Any second now it would smash the glass and finish him off...

There was a crash. The sub rocked. The silver spike thrust through the broken plexiglass. More water surged in. Then the spike withdrew and the water poured in faster. Max forced his way against the torrent to the opening. If he could just squeeze through the gap...

The pressure pushed him back. He took one last deep breath, and then the water was

over his head.

He clamped his mouth shut. He struggled forwards, feeling the pressure in his lungs build.

Something gripped his arms, but it wasn't the squid's tentacle – it was a pair of hands, pulling him through the hole. The broken plexiglass scraped his sides – and then he was through.

The monster was nowhere to be seen. In the dim underwater light, he made out the face of his rescuer. It was the Merryn girl, and next to her was a large silver swordfish.

She smiled at him.

Max couldn't smile back. He'd been saved from a metal coffin, only to swap it for a watery one. The pressure of the ocean squeezed him on every side. His lungs felt as though they were bursting.

He thrashed his limbs, rising upwards.

He looked to where he thought the surface was, but saw nothing, only endless water. His cheeks puffed with the effort to hold in air. He let some of it out slowly, but it only made him want to breathe in more.

He knew he had no chance. He was too deep, he'd never make it to the surface. Soon he'd no longer be able to hold his breath. The water would swirl into his lungs and he'd die here, at the bottom of the sea. *Just like my mother*, he thought.

The Merryn girl rose up beside him, reached out and put her hands on his neck. Warmth seemed to flow from her fingers. Then the warmth turned to pain. What was happening? It got worse and worse, until he felt as if his throat was being ripped open. Was she trying to kill him?

He struggled in panic, trying to push her off. His mouth opened and water rushed in.

———

That was it. He was going to die.

Then he realised something – the water was cool and sweet. He sucked it down into his lungs. Nothing had ever tasted so good.

He was breathing underwater!

He put his hands to his neck and found two soft, gill-like openings where the Merryn

girl had touched him. His eyes widened in astonishment.

The girl smiled.

There was something else strange. Max found he could see more clearly. The water seemed lighter and thinner. He made out the shapes of underwater plants, rock formations and shoals of fish in the distance, which had been invisible before. And he didn't feel as if the ocean was crushing him any more.

Is this what it's like to be a Merryn? he wondered.

"I'm Lia," said the girl. "And this is Spike." She patted the swordfish on the back and it nuzzled against her.

"Hi, I'm Max." He clapped his hand to his mouth in shock. He was speaking the same strange language of sighs and whistles he'd heard the girl use when he first met her –

but now it made sense, as if he was born to speak it.

"What have you done to me?"

"Saved your life," said Lia. "You're welcome, by the way."

"Oh – don't think I'm not grateful – I am. But – you've turned me into a Merryn?"

The girl laughed. "Not exactly – but I've given you some Merryn powers. You can breath underwater, speak our language, and your senses are much stronger. Come on – we need to get away from here. The Cybersquid may come back."

In one graceful movement she slipped onto Spike's back. Max clambered on behind her.

"Hold tight," Lia said. "Spike – let's go!"

Max put his arms around the Merryn's waist. He was jerked backwards as the swordfish shot off through the water, but he managed to hold on.

———

They raced above underwater forests of gently waving fronds, and hills and valleys of rock. Max saw giant crabs scuttling over the seabed. Undersea creatures loomed up – jellyfish, an octopus, a school of dolphins – but Spike nimbly swerved round them.

"Where are we going?" Max asked.

"You'll see," Lia said over her shoulder.

"I need to find my dad," Max said. The crazy things that had happened in the last few moments had driven his father from his mind. Now it all came flooding back. Was his dad gone for good? "We have to do something! That monster's got my dad – and my dogbot too!"

"It's not the squid who wants your father. It's the Professor who's *controlling* the squid. I tried to warn you back at the city – but you wouldn't listen."

"I didn't understand you then!"

"You Breathers don't try to understand – that's your whole problem!"

"I'm trying now. What is that monster? And who is the Professor?"

"I'll explain everything when we arrive."

"Arrive where?"

The seabed suddenly fell away. A steep valley sloped down, leading way, way deeper than the ocean ridge Aquora was built on. The swordfish dived. The water grew darker.

Far below, Max saw a faint yellow glimmer. As he watched it grew bigger and brighter, until it became a vast undersea city of golden-glinting rock rushing up towards them. There were towers, spires, domes, bridges, courtyards, squares, gardens. A city as big as Aquora, and far more beautiful, at the bottom of the sea.

Max gasped in amazement. The water was dark, but the city emitted a glow of its own

– a warm phosphorescent light that spilled
from the many windows. The rock sparkled.
Orange, pink and scarlet corals and seashells
decorated the walls in intricate patterns.

———

"This is – amazing!" he said.

Lia turned round and smiled at him. "It's our home," she said. "Sumara!"

———